CONTENTS

YOU CHOOSE

MATCH DAY
FOOTBALL

AN INTERACTIVE SPORTS STORY

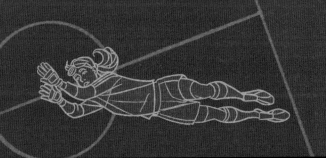

BY BRANDON TERRELL
ILLUSTRATED BY FRAN BUENO

Raintree is an imprint of Capstone Global Library Limited, a company incorporated in England and Wales having its registered office at 264 Banbury Road, Oxford, OX2 7DY – Registered company number: 6695582

www.raintree.co.uk
myorders@raintree.co.uk

Edited by Angie Kaelberer
Designed by Kayla Rossow
Original illustrations © Capstone Global Library Limited 2022
Picture research by Eric Gohl
Production by Katy LaVigne
Originated by Capstone Global Library Ltd
Printed and bound in India

978 1 3982 1586 3

British Library Cataloguing in Publication Data
A full catalogue record for this book is available from the British Library.

ABOUT YOUR MATCH

YOU are a talented footballer known for working hard and using your athletic ability and instincts to help your team win. But you're on a new team now, which just happens to be the top rival of your former team. Can you put your old loyalties aside to help lead your new team to victory?

Chapter 1 sets the scene. Then you choose which path to read. Follow the directions at the bottom of the page as you read. The decisions you make will change your outcome. After you've finished one path, go back and read the others for new perspectives and more adventures.

CHAPTER 1

NEW TEAM, SAME RIVALRY

"This just doesn't look right."

You're staring at yourself in the full-length mirror in your bedroom. Around it, the walls are cluttered with posters of your favourite professional players. The rest of the room contains nothing more than an unmade bed and a load of cardboard boxes.

You shake your head. You can't believe the football top you're wearing. It has a black stripe down the middle and across the front is the word *Jaguars*.

You shake your head. "We had to go and move, didn't we?" you mutter.

Turn the page.

After your mum was recently promoted at work, your family moved to a bigger house in a new neighbourhood. The only problem? You also had to change schools.

And not to just any school. And not just at any time of year. No, you moved near the end of the football season to the school on the other side of the city. Your crosstown rivals. You went from being an East Bridgeton Badger – the top team in the city – to a West Bridgeton Jaguar, your fiercest rival. And today, the two teams face off in the semi-final.

The pitch at West Bridgeton Middle School is teeming with people when you arrive. Everyone wants to see the teams battle it out. You just never thought you'd be on the other side of the battlefield.

As you get out of the car and sling your kit bag over your shoulder, you can't help but put your head down. It feels like everyone's watching and whispering.

When you get to the bench, Coach Stevens is waiting. "Are you ready for the match of your life?" she asks.

You nod, but say nothing.

The rest of your teammates are lacing up their boots or dribbling balls on the grass. Among them is Malia, the tallest player on the team. You also see Hannah, who has quick eyes and a killer bend in her kick. Jasmine, the team goalkeeper, is there too.

They all look at you when you arrive. You know what their stares mean.

Turn the page.

You were an enemy. Worse, a Badger. And here you are, on their team. Playing in a game that will determine if the team moves on to the final.

You sit on the bench and lace up your boots in silence. The ref blows a whistle.

"All right, let's get going!" Coach Stevens yells. Your teammates start to gather their things. Quickly, you pull Coach Stevens aside.

"What's up?" she asks.

"I know I'm new," you reply, "and the rest of the team has played a whole season together. Plus," you nod across the pitch at the Badgers, "I used to be one of them. I just wanted you to know, as a way to show everyone I'm a team player, I'm cool playing any position on the pitch you want."

Coach Stevens nods. "I like that attitude," she says. "Where do *you* think you'd be best at playing?"

To be the team's striker, turn to page 13.

To opt to play left winger, turn to page 39.

To decide you're best defending the team at wingback, turn to page 71.

CHAPTER 2

STRIKING ON THE FRONT LINES

"The new girl's gonna play where?" Hannah asks incredulously.

"You heard me," Coach Stevens replies. "Striker. And you'll be her left wing."

You played striker for the Badgers, so when Coach Stevens asked you where you felt comfortable playing, the answer was obvious. As striker, you have the best chance to score and prove to your new team that you're on the pitch to win. After all, it is your old team and friends you're up against, and you know their moves better than anyone.

Turn the page.

But this was also the response you'd expected from your new teammates. They don't trust you yet.

"We're a team out there," Coach Stevens says sharply. "No matter what position we play."

The referee blows a whistle, signalling the teams to start the match. You can see the looks your teammates are giving each other. They don't agree with Coach Stevens's decision. And as they start to walk out onto the pitch, they already look deflated and defeated.

It's your job as striker to lead from the front. But how can you do it if they don't trust you? You could show them your leadership on the pitch. Or you can stop the feeling of mistrust before the match by talking to them.

To pull the team aside now and talk to them, go to page 15.

To show them leadership on the pitch, turn to page 34.

"Hey, everyone," you say. "Huddle up!"

The team looks over at you. They appear surprised. But they jog over, and you all cluster together.

"Look," you say. "I know it's weird having an ex-Badger as a member of the team. But we're here to win this match, and we can only do that together. I'm with you." You hold out your hand, palm down. "Are you with me?"

They glance at each other. Then Jasmine places her gloved hand on yours. Others follow. Hannah is last. "We are," they say.

"Then 'Go, Jaguars' on three," you reply. "One . . . two . . . three . . ."

"GO, JAGUARS!"

The pep talk seems to work!

Turn the page.

As the game begins, you feel the energy as the Jaguars race up and down the pitch. But you can also sense the Badgers' aggression. Especially in their striker, Zoe Moore.

"Watch out, traitor," Zoe says as you run down the pitch together. "I'm coming for you."

The ball soars in your direction, and you manage to stop it with your left foot. You zip past Zoe. You're on the counter-attack, dribbling swiftly into your zone. The middle of the pitch is wide open. But so is Hannah to your right.

To pass the ball to Hannah, go to page 17.
To take the shot yourself, turn to page 21.

The Badger goalkeeper is crouched, eyes focused on you. Hannah throws up her hand.

In one swift move, you hook the ball with your toe and rocket it over to Hannah. She thrusts out her chest and the ball hits her perfectly, landing at her feet. She dribbles up the pitch and unleashes a kick that bends high and right.

The Badger goalie is thrown off by your pass and can't recover. The ball sails into the net. The Jaguars have scored the first goal of the match!

As you jog back to midfield together, Hannah holds out her fist. "Nice assist, newbie," she says with a smirk.

"Thanks." You bump her fist back.

Hannah's goal is a huge boost for the Jaguars' confidence.

Turn the page.

Your other winger, Bao Khang, uses her mad ball-dribbling skills to carve her way down the pitch and score a second goal for the Jaguars. Your new team has skills, that's for sure.

But Zoe Moore is doing what she can to remind you of your past. "You used to play for the best," she taunts. "Now look at you."

"Look at the scoreboard, Zoe," you reply.

The ball is headed your way. A Badger defender races after the ball, but you think you have a chance at getting there first.

To let the Badger defender get the ball, go to page 19.
To go for the open ball, turn to page 28.

You slow down. A collision is the last thing you need.

The defender gets to the ball and dribbles it down the pitch. She passes it to Zoe, who passes to a winger racing down the left side.

Turn the page.

It looks like she's going to get a shot on goal. From nowhere, the Jaguars' quick midfielder, Luna Barnes, is there to stand in her way.

Thwump!

Luna knocks the ball free, shattering the Badgers' chances.

The Badgers have a never-give-up attitude, though. The next time they have the ball, their passing skills are on full display. Zoe bends a kick over Jasmine's outstretched hands.

"Goal!" the ref shouts. They've cut the lead to one.

It's nearly the end of the first half. Your teammates are getting tired. Hannah is sweating. Malia is sucking in air, hand on her cramped side. You know you need to do something to get your team back in the match.

Turn to page 30.

Yes, Hannah is open. But the middle of the pitch is right there in front of you! The chance to prove your worth to your new team is too tempting. So you dribble the ball up the pitch, ignoring Hannah's shouts and waves.

You flip the ball from one foot to the other, doing your best to deceive the Badger goalkeeper, Mara Rinehart. But Mara knows you too well. She smirks as you line up and drill the ball at the goal.

Mara dives right, perfectly snagging your shot out of the air!

As she overhand throws the ball back into play, you hear Malia behind you. "Ball hog," she mutters.

Turn the page.

The Jaguars are definitely not gelling as a team, and you feel like a spanner in their well-oiled machine. A sloppy pass from Malia to Hannah is easily intercepted. Bao trips a Badger player accidentally and gives away a free kick. You're supposed to be leading from the front, but nothing seems to be going according to plan.

Steffi Powers, the Jaguars' other main defender, gets the ball. She boots it high into the air. It's sailing right towards you. But you're not the only player nearby. You could try to jump up and head the ball. Or you could anticipate a pass and slip towards the goal.

To back away from the incoming ball, go to page 23.
To jump up and head the ball, turn to page 29.

You step back, keeping your eyes on the ball. It comes towards Malia, who had the same idea as you and jumps to head the ball.

It bounces off her forehead . . . right towards you!

You knock the pass down with the inside of your left foot, then dribble up the pitch. Mara is favouring the left side of the goal, so you fake her out and shoot at the upper-right corner of the net.

Swish!

"Great shot!" Malia concedes. Maybe her attitude towards you is changing.

The Badgers up their aggression. Each time you and Zoe both go for the ball, you jostle into each other.

Turn the page.

In the second half, the Badgers level the score. The Jaguars are exhausted and in desperate need of a breather. When the referee halts the game to allow a Badgers player to receive treatment, Coach Stevens gathers everyone round.

"All right, Jaguars," Coach Stevens says. "Stay calm. Don't play their games, and keep a level head. You've got this!"

The team members nod and take deep breaths. The pep talk was just what you needed.

As the second half progresses, you see the Jaguars have regained some strength. When the Badgers go on the counter-attack and Zoe takes a great shot on goal, Jasmine is there to stop it.

Jasmine swings the ball out to Jaguar midfielder Luna Barnes, who passes to Malia. Malia sees you in the middle of the pitch and slips a great pass to you.

You see Bao up ahead. But this is also a great chance to score a goal.

To pass to Bao, turn to page 26.
To take the ball up the pitch yourself, turn to page 30.

You've got a wide-open path in front of you now, but spy Zoe out of the corner of your eye. You decide it's best to pass the ball off to Bao.

The pass lands perfectly in front of her, leading Bao right towards the goal. Mara crouches, prepared. Bao sizes up the shot and lets it fly.

Thwack!

Mara dives in front of the ball, and it slaps off her gloved hands. She leaps up and snatches the ball before you can get to it and take a follow-up shot.

When the final whistle blows, the score is still level. You're going to extra time!

Extra time is more of a struggle. Neither team is able to score, so it goes to a penalty shoot-out.

"In the shoot-out, five players from each team

will take a free shot at the goal. The only question is where you'll fit in this new line-up of strong Jaguar players.

Coach Stevens answers the question for you. She points at you and says, "You're up first."

To agree with Coach Stevens and kick first, turn to page 32.

To tell her you'd prefer to kick last, turn to page 33.

The Badgers are playing fast and hard, so you decide you need to as well. You lower your head and race towards the ball.

You get there at the same time as the Badger defender, colliding with a loud smack. Her elbow slams into your ribs. You try to breathe, but the wind has been knocked out of you.

Your studs gouge into the defender's ankle. Your own ankle twists, and another jolt of pain hits you. This time, you fall to the grass.

"Come on," Coach Stevens says as she helps you to your feet. "You need to sit down until we can get that ankle looked at."

You take a seat on the bench and watch in pain as the Badgers come back to win the game.

THE END

To follow another path, turn to page 11.
To learn more about football, turn to page 103.

It bothered you that Malia called you a ball hog. You want to prove her wrong. As the ball spins towards you, you leap up to hit it with your head and pass it to her.

There's just one problem. Malia had the same idea! She jumps up, and the two of you collide in mid-air. You both fall to the grass as a Badger slips in and takes the ball away.

"What were you thinking?" Malia shouts.

"I'm sorry," you say weakly.

At the other end of the pitch, the Badgers score. Malia and your other teammates look upset with you, and it shows on the pitch. You barely get the ball for the rest of the match. And the Badgers run away with an easy victory.

THE END
To follow another path, turn to page 11.
To learn more about football, turn to page 103.

You take the ball up the pitch yourself. Zoe cuts you off, but you're able to slip past her. When you're close to the goal, you fake a pass to Hannah but take the shot yourself. It sizzles into the top corner of the net!

"Great shot!" Hannah and Malia say together. The team is invigorated by this goal, and you've done your job gaining their trust.

The Jaguars' confidence doesn't waver. Before long, Hannah has added another goal, stretching your lead.

There's not much time left on the clock, and the angry Badgers know it. They push and shove, struggling. You can't believe this was the style of game you used to play.

When good teamwork and solid passing lead to another goal by Malia, you smile. This new team? They're a great group to play alongside.

With the lead and a loud, packed crowd, you and the Jaguars easily hand the Badgers a solid defeat.

THE END

To follow another path, turn to page 11.
To learn more about football, turn to page 103.

You nod. "Yes, Coach," you say.

As the first Jaguar to kick, it's your job to set the bar for the team.

With a ball tucked under one arm, you stride onto the pitch. You put the ball down and prepare to kick.

You step back, eye the goal and pick your spot. Then you race up and boot the ball with the inside of your right foot. It hooks left, curling towards the corner of the goal.

Mara dives. The ball strikes her forearms and falls. You missed!

Unfortunately, yours is not the only shot she blocks. By the time the shoot-out has ended, the Badgers have won 3–1.

THE END

To follow another path, turn to page 11.
To learn more about football, turn to page 103.

You step back and hold up your hands. "I think someone else should go first, Coach," you say. "Set the bar and all."

"Fine," Coach Stevens says. "Hannah, you're up."

"Got it," Hannah replies. She grabs a ball and jogs onto the pitch.

You watch as Hannah confidently scores the first goal of the shoot-out. Bao follows with another, and Malia adds a third. The Badgers keep pace, though. So when it's your turn to kick last, the shoot-out score is level.

You line up your shot. Mara looks unsure. You aim left, but fake her out and kick to the right. The ball sizzles past her. The Jaguars win!

THE END

To follow another path, turn to page 11.
To learn more about football, turn to page 103.

You see the looks passing between your teammates as you take the pitch to start the match. You get it. You're new, and you're playing striker. How could this possibly go well?

You consider huddling up, giving them a pep talk. But it's better if you *show* your team that you can play.

The Badger striker, Zoe Moore, is waiting for you in midfield. She used to be your friend. Now she just smirks at you. "Good to see you," she says mockingly. She's trying to get under your skin. "Have a great game."

It's clear from the start that the Jaguars aren't gelling as a team. You attempt to pass the ball up to Hannah, but your aim is off and it sails past her, out of play.

"Come on, newbie!" Hannah shouts, slapping her hands together in frustration.

Turn the page.

You don't know what to do. You want to help your new team, but whatever you do, it seems to backfire. You feel like a failure.

This isn't me, you tell yourself. *I can do this. I can help the Jaguars win.* You take a deep breath and try to refocus on the match.

For a while, your efforts to calm yourself seem to help. Late in the first half, as you bring the ball up the pitch, you see Hannah and Bao are both struggling to get open. Hannah breaks free, but isn't looking your way. But it's the perfect chance to pass to her!

"Hannah!" you shout, kicking the ball in her direction.

Hannah glances over at you, but it's a second too late. As she lunges for the ball, she becomes tangled with a Badger defender. To your horror, they both fall to the ground in a heap.

Hannah moans in pain as Coach Stevens and the team rush to her side. As she passes you, Malia asks, "Did you do that on purpose?"

"What? No."

Her eyes say she doesn't believe you.

You can only watch as Hannah is helped off the pitch. Your team won't be giving you the benefit of the doubt now. And even worse, all the Jaguars seem to lose their confidence. It's no surprise to any of you when the Badgers win the game.

THE END

To follow another path, turn to page 11.
To learn more about football, turn to page 103.

CHAPTER 3

SPEEDY WINGER

You mull over Coach Stevens's question. "It's not my place to play striker," you say. "Not for my first match. But I'm fine playing forward. I'll take left wing, if that's cool."

"Done," Coach Stevens says. "Hannah, you're striker."

The Jaguars jog out onto the pitch. You're nervous about facing your old team, and you can see they're glaring at you. Especially Zoe Moore, the team's striker. "Be careful," you tell the other Jaguars. "The Badgers love to be aggressive and to get the other team penalized with yellow and red cards."

"Good to know," Hannah says.

Turn the page.

As the game starts, the Badgers are bumping and playing hard. Zoe shakes past Hannah, using her left hand to shove off where the referee won't notice.

"Hey!" Hannah shouts.

Moments later, it happens again. This time, Malia is knocked over while fighting for the ball. Again, the ref doesn't see what's happening.

You start to think that you'll need to play as aggressively as the Badgers to win the match. But should you?

To play as aggressively as the Badgers, go to page 41.
To continue playing Jaguar-style, turn to page 50.

If Zoe and the Badgers are going to play rough, then you're going to have to play at their level.

You race down the pitch. The Badger defender goes after the ball at the same time. You bump and nudge. Not enough to give away a free kick, but enough to let the Badgers know you remember how you used to play.

Early in the game, Hannah and Zoe tangle for the ball. It breaks free and heads in Malia's direction.

Malia sees you and sends a skittering pass in your direction. The ball is in front of you, and you're not sure you'll be able to reach it. The defender races to your side, keeping pace. You're both trying desperately to reach the ball before it goes out of play.

To let the ball go out of play, turn to page 42.
To try to reach the ball and pass it, turn to page 45.

You know you won't reach the ball before it goes out of play. The Badger defender takes a swipe at it. Her toe hooks the ball but doesn't stop it.

"Jaguar ball!" the ref shouts.

You take the throw-in, holding the ball high over your head. Hannah dashes past a stumbling defender, and you hurl the ball at her.

Hannah deftly dribbles up the pitch She spies Bao, the other Jaguar winger, across the way and passes it over.

Bao immediately shoots.

Swish!

The ball hits the back of the net! "Goal!" the ref shouts.

The Jaguars have the lead. And as the game continues, Malia is able to add a second goal.

This doesn't sit well with the Badgers. You can see the fire and intensity in their eyes. As Zoe takes the ball up the pitch, you spy Jaguar midfielder Luna Barnes rushing up to meet her. Zoe drops a shoulder, and Luna collides with her.

"Free kick!" the ref says, holding up a yellow card to Zoe.

"Oh, come on!" Zoe protests. "*She* ran into *me*."

Luna hobbles off the pitch. She's injured but should be able to make it back into the game.

The Jaguars get the ball back. After some fancy passing, Malia goes on the counter-attack. A Badger defender catches up to her, and the two tangle for the ball.

"Watch out!" you hear Malia shout.

Turn the page.

The Badger falls to the grass. This time it's your team that gives away the free kick.

Things are starting to get out of control. You look to Coach Stevens, hoping she sees it too.

To get your coach's attention,
turn to page 55.

To trust that the team will pull itself together,
turn to page 57.

You're playing fast and hard and won't let the ball go out of play.

You race after it at the same time as the Badger defender. She gives you a light shove in the back.

"Oof!" you say as you stumble forward. Your right elbow strikes the defender in the chest, knocking her over. The ref blows the whistle.

Tweet! "Foul," she calls, pointing at you.

The call is unfair, though. You feel like you need to plead your case with the ref.

To accept the foul call, turn to page 46.
To plead your case with the referee, turn to page 59.

You open your mouth to protest against the call, then immediately close it. No, arguing isn't the way to win this match.

The Badgers have a corner kick. As the ball comes into play, Zoe snags it but fails to score.

Time is running out, and the score is level! Seconds are left on the clock. Zoe rockets a shot at goal, but Jasmine blocks it. She scoops up the ball and lobs it in your direction.

The Badgers have a strong line of defenders coming at you as you dribble the ball past midfield. You're very aware that time is ticking away.

Out of the corner of your eye, you see Bao. It's a long pass across the pitch to her, but she's more open than you.

You have a split second to decide.

To make the risky pass to Bao, turn to page 48.
To take the shot yourself, turn to page 61.

The Badgers in front of you mean business. Bao has a much better angle than you on the goal, even though she's across the pitch. It's a dangerous pass to make, but there are only seconds left on the clock. You need to decide *now*.

"Bao! Heads up!" You twist your body and uncork a pass that sails quickly across the pitch towards Bao. And she's ready for it.

But so are the Badgers.

A Badger defender peels off, racing to the ball and intercepting it from Bao.

Time runs out before she can do anything, though. You're heading into extra time!

"I know you're tired," Coach Stevens says as you prepare for extra time. "But I have faith in you. Dig deep and find that strength. Got it?"

"Yes, Coach!" the team shouts in unison.

The game has been gruelling, and extra time is no different. It's a long, tiring battle. Your legs strain as you run down the pitch. They feel like jelly – as if you could fall over at any second.

For most of extra time, neither team gets any advantage. Jasmine and Mara, the two goalies, stop every shot that comes their way.

But then, as Jasmine lobs a pass to Hannah, the ball bounces past the Jaguar striker. It skitters across the grass, right towards Zoe! Zoe meets it and dribbles effortlessly on the counter-attack.

You race to catch up. You're the closest player to Zoe. She's near the goal and about to shoot. Jasmine looks tired, and you're not sure she'll be able to stop Zoe's shot this time.

To trust Jasmine to make the save, turn to page 62.
To try to block Zoe's kick yourself, turn to page 63.

You're used to the way the Badgers play – hard, aggressive, relentless. But that doesn't mean your new team has to play that way. They've got their own method, and you're a part of *their* team now. So you play that way too.

And it works. The team is gelling, and you're a big part of that. Your job as winger is to pass the ball and get your team in a scoring position.

Hannah brings the ball up the pitch. As she does, you dash past the Badger defender, who's caught between following you and going after Hannah. This is the best chance you've had to score, and you want to give the Jaguars the early lead. You throw your hand up. "Over here!"

Hannah sees you and passes it over. But the pass is high, and you're not sure how to stop the ball.

To jump up and head the ball, go to page 51.
To use your chest to control the ball, turn to page 53.

You leap into the air just as the ball reaches you.

Smack!

The ball bounces perfectly off the crown of your head. It sails over Zoe and a second Badger defender and lands in front of Bao, the other Jaguar winger.

Bao easily slips a shot past Mara Rinehart, the Badger goalkeeper.

"Nice shot!" you say, bumping fists with Bao.

"Nice pass!" she replies.

The Jaguars hold the slim lead through the first half.

The second half remains a tight battle. Hannah manages to score, but so does Zoe. The Jaguars' lead is still one goal, and time is ticking away.

Turn the page.

With just moments left on the clock, the ball heads your way. It's flying high again, and you have a chance to do a difficult mid-air kick. The ball's position isn't ideal. If you nail it, though, you'll surprise the goalie and give the Jaguars a strong lead with almost no time for the Badgers to come back.

To let the ball land, turn to page 65.
To attempt the mid-air kick, turn to page 67.

You could try something that'll make the crowd roar, but that's not the smart move. Not in this situation. So instead you decide to use your chest to stop the ball.

But as the ball reaches you, you realize you've mistimed it.

Thwack!

The ball strikes your left palm.

The ref blows the whistle, and the ball goes back to the Badgers.

This move shifts the game's momentum in the Badgers' favour. Zoe is able to score near the end of the first half. In the second half, there's a flurry of goals. The game is level.

Turn the page.

Less than a minute is left on the clock. Hannah brings the ball up the pitch. She sees you open on the left side and passes you the ball. You take it, dribbling towards the goal. The defender, who was guarding Malia, hurries your way. But you have a clear shot and a chance to go ahead.

To aim for the left side of the goal, turn to page 68.
To aim for the right side of the goal, turn to page 69.

Things are getting away from you. If you're not careful, the Badgers will take over the match completely. You turn to the bench and signal Coach Stevens.

The next time the game is halted for a player to receive treatment, Coach Stevens calls the team together. They look tired and in pain.

"Catch your breath, everyone," Coach Stevens says. "Get some water. We've got this."

You nod. "Remember to play smart," you tell the team. "Don't fall for their tricks, and don't get too wild so you give away a free kick."

The team nods in agreement.

When the ref blows the whistle and the game resumes, you can already tell the pep talk was worth it. Jasmine is standing a bit taller, and the pain in Hannah's side has gone away.

Turn the page.

The Jaguars look ready to play.

The Jaguars play a strong second half, not caving to the Badgers' intense play. The ref has also caught on to their tactics, as Zoe gives away a couple of free kicks late in the game.

With minutes left on the clock, Hannah takes a high pass and performs a perfect header, knocking the ball past the goalkeeper. Bao adds another goal late in the game, securing the victory for the Jaguars.

As the Badgers slump off the pitch, you and your new team celebrate a strong victory!

THE END

To follow another path, turn to page 11.
To learn more about football, turn to page 103.

It's OK, you think. *We've got this!*

Instead of signalling your concerns to Coach Stevens, you gather the Jaguars. "We can do this!" you say, bumping fists with Bao.

The Badgers are relentless, though. As the second half starts, they score a quick flurry of goals, three in all. They've taken the lead!

It looks like the Jaguars are not used to the same level of intensity as the Badgers, and they're wearing down.

When the ref halts the game so a Badgers player can receive treatment, Coach Stevens calls the team over to the sideline.

Jasmine, the goalkeeper, looks completely worn out. And she's not alone.

"I don't know how much more I've got," Hannah says, grabbing at her side and gasping.

Turn the page.

It's clear the Badgers have you right where they want you. As time trickles away, they score another goal past the tired Jasmine.

The Jaguars are now too far behind to come back. It looks like you'll have to wait until next season to beat the Badgers.

THE END

To follow another path, turn to page 11.
To learn more about football, turn to page 103.

"Come on, ref!" you say, running over to her. "There's no way I elbowed her on purpose!"

The ref just looks at you and says nothing.

"It's not fair and you know it!" You're letting your anger get the better of you. It doesn't help that Zoe is standing behind the ref with a sly smirk on her face.

Turn the page.

59

Bao hurries over. You think she's there to back you up. Instead, she stands between you and the ref.

"Hey," she says to you, "chill out."

Bao drags you away from the ref. You can feel your heart thudding against your rib cage. You got out of hand, and you'll have to deal with the consequences.

Coach Stevens glares at you as you reach the bench. "Arguing with the ref is *not* how we play," she says. "Find a place on the bench and warm it. Your game is over."

You slump onto the bench. This wasn't how your first match as a Jaguar was supposed to go. You can only watch as the Badgers come back to dominate the match and win.

THE END

To follow another path, turn to page 11.
To learn more about football, turn to page 103.

Yes, your old teammates are coming up fast. They're in your face. But you find a gap and dribble through them.

It's just you and Mara Rinehart, the Badger goalkeeper.

You unleash a bending shot that sails high. For a second, you're afraid it'll soar over the goal. But it catches the corner, just out of Mara's grasp.

You did it!

The whistle blows, and you and the Jaguars are victorious!

THE END

To follow another path, turn to page 11.
To learn more about football, turn to page 103.

Sure, Jasmine's tired. But you've come to trust your new teammate.

Zoe shoots, and sure enough, Jasmine snags the ball out of the air.

"Great save!" you shout.

Jasmine hurls the ball down the pitch, where a waiting Hannah takes it. She dribbles past a defender and takes her own shot.

Swish!

"Goal! Jaguars win!" the ref bellows.

The team races out onto the pitch. You've done it. You've beaten your old team and made a lasting memory with your new one.

THE END

To follow another path, turn to page 11.
To learn more about football, turn to page 103.

It's been a long match. Jasmine's tired. You can see it in her eyes. And you've got a chance to make sure the Badgers won't be able to score.

So you take it.

You speed up, catching Zoe as she reaches the front of the goal. However, as you go to kick the ball, your leg strikes her below the knee, knocking her to the ground.

"Penalty," the ref shouts.

Zoe stands, brushing herself off. You can't believe you made such a stupid mistake. And because it occurred in the penalty box, Zoe will have a penalty kick.

Turn the page.

The ref drops the ball, and Zoe lines up for the penalty. She stutter-steps, fakes right, then kicks high and to the left.

The ball sails past Jasmine, right into the goal.

The match is over. The Badgers celebrate their extra-time win as you sulk off the pitch in defeat.

THE END

To follow another path, turn to page 11.
To learn more about football, turn to page 103.

You decide the ball is too high for a successful mid-air kick. There's no way you're going to attempt a bad kick. You wait for the ball to land.

When it does, you notice you have a clear shot on goal. You take the shot.

Whoosh! The ball flies past Mara, hitting the back of the net.

You've extended the Jaguars' lead with just seconds to go. The Badgers don't have enough time to catch up. Jaguars win the match! You're going to the final!

THE END

To follow another path, turn to page 11.
To learn more about football, turn to page 103.

You leap into the air, swivelling your hips and kicking the ball. It's not perfect, though, and neither is your landing. As you come back down, your ankle twists in the grass.

"Ouch!" Pain jolts up your leg, and you crumple to the ground.

The team rallies around you, helping you limp off the pitch. When you reach the bench, Coach Stevens says, "Put some ice on that ankle. You need to sit out and rest it."

As you watch, the Badgers rally late, coming from behind to beat your new team.

THE END

To follow another path, turn to page 11.
To learn more about football, turn to page 103.

You're a right-footed kicker. And Mara, the goalie, knows that. So she'll be anticipating a kick to the right side of the goal.

So you aim left.

Mara is ready, though. She dives and snags the ball out of mid-air.

"I'm open!" Zoe shouts from the far side of the pitch.

Mara hurls the ball in her direction, and Zoe takes it up the pitch. She doesn't have the same bad luck as you, though. She sneaks a goal past Jasmine, breaking the tie.

As time runs out, the Badgers are victorious.

THE END

To follow another path, turn to page 11.
To learn more about football, turn to page 103.

Mara crouches. She's leaning slightly to the left, so you're aiming for the right side of the net.

Whump!

You kick the ball with the side of your foot, sending it to the right side of the goal. Mara, off-balance, tries to dive that way. But she comes up short, and the ball sails over her head.

You did it!

As time runs out, the Jaguars win by your last-second goal. You helped your new team win, and you can't stop smiling.

THE END
To follow another path, turn to page 11.
To learn more about football, turn to page 103.

CHAPTER 4

TURNING UP THE DEFENSIVE HEAT

"So what'll it be?" Coach Stevens asks.

"I know how aggressively the Badgers play," you say. "So I'll play wingback and defend against them."

Coach Stevens nods. "All right," she says. "Hit the pitch, team!"

As you take to the pitch, Jasmine sidles up next to you. "Glad you're back on defence with me," she says. "I remember last season, when you hooked that goal past me." She shakes her head. "I lost sleep over that shot. So I'm happy you're a Jaguar now."

Turn the page.

As the game begins, you notice the Badgers playing aggressively. Zoe Moore, their striker, is swift and relentless. Within the first few minutes of play, she finds a way to break past you and score a goal.

"How's the new team treating you?" she asks smugly. She used to be your friend. Apparently, that's changed. She's set on humiliating you and Steffi Powers, the other Jaguar defender.

Moments later, the Badgers are attacking again. Zoe and her wingers are racing towards you. Steffi stumbles, and Luna Barnes, a Jaguar midfielder, is on the far side of the pitch. You have to decide who to attack.

To focus your attention on Zoe, go to page 73.
To anticipate Zoe passing the ball, turn to page 83.

Zoe is a striker and the strongest Badger on the pitch. You race over to cover her.

But your haste in reaching Zoe is exactly what she wants. With fast footwork, she flips the ball to the open winger. The winger scores, and the Jaguars are quickly down 2–0.

Come on, you tell yourself. *You have to focus.*

As Zoe jogs back to midfield, she comes up behind you. "Hey, I don't remember you playing this badly when you were a Badger!" You try to remain emotionless, but inside, you're fired up.

Just before the end of the first half, Hannah scores. This cuts the Badgers' lead to 2–1. The game is fast and intense, more than you thought it would be. By the time the first half ends, you're sucking in air and in need of a break.

Turn the page.

"Everyone in," Coach Stevens says. She waves you all over. "That was a wild first half. But we're still in this match. One goal is all it takes to shift the momentum. Are you ready to go out there and take this game back from them?"

"Yes, Coach!" the team bellows.

As you prepare to walk out onto the pitch, Coach Stevens stops you. "Have a seat," she says. "You look worn out so I'm going to make a substitution."

To plead with Coach to let you play, go to page 75.
To start the second half on the bench, turn to page 79.

"Come on, Coach," you plead. "I'm good to go. Trust me."

Coach Stevens eyes you, then nods. "OK," she says.

As the second half starts, you feel good. Zoe tries to dribble the ball past you, but you block it and send the ball forward to Hannah in the middle of the pitch.

But just then you feel light-headed. The football pitch seems to be spinning around you.

You shake your head, and things come back into focus.

The ball comes skittering back towards you. You chase after it, but the dizzy feeling returns. You stumble and fall, sliding across the grass.

The ref stops play, and a sub hurries onto the pitch to take your place.

Turn the page.

You can't blame Coach Stevens. You should have accepted being taken off at half time.

As you sit on the bench, regaining your strength, Zoe slips another goal past Jasmine, increasing the Badgers' lead. Frustrated, you sit the game out until Coach Stevens surprisingly decides to make another substitution and put you back onto the pitch. You have been given an unlikely second chance!

There's a bit of time left on the clock, though, and you're down a couple of goals.

Two Badgers race down the pitch, passing the ball back and forth. You've got your eyes on Zoe. It looks like she's about to pass the ball.

To anticipate her pass, go to page 77.
To stick with covering Zoe, turn to page 88.

You have played alongside Zoe before, so you know this move. But then, she's also aware of that fact.

You shift back, waiting for the pass as Steffi hustles over to help. And yes! Just as you expect, Zoe kicks the ball towards the winger. But you're right there to intercept it.

"Luna! Heads up!" You pass the ball over to her on the left side, and Luna brings it past midfield. You watch as she then passes to Malia. Malia sends the ball past the Badger goalkeeper.

"Yes!" you shout, pumping your fist.

Momentum has shifted back in the Jaguars' favour. You can feel the energy as the team huddles together before the game restarts. But there isn't much time left on the clock, and you're still down a goal.

Turn the page.

The two teams battle back and forth, neither getting a clear shot on goal. You look up at the clock. Less than a minute left.

"Jasmine!" Coach Stevens calls. "Move up into the Badger's penalty box!" She waves the goalie up the pitch.

She's sending the goalkeeper up into the attack!

That leaves you with an empty net but also gives the Jaguars one more player trying to score.

To join Jasmine in attack, turn to page 89.
To decide to stay on defence, turn to page 90.

Coach Stevens is right. You definitely need a rest.

You start the second half on the bench, watching as the Badgers score again, putting them ahead by two goals. Then Hannah finds a way to slip past Zoe, sending a kick high into the upper-right corner of the net.

Swish!

"All right," Coach Stevens says, waving for you. "I'm going to put you back on. Go get 'em!"

You hurry back onto the pitch. You can't believe you've been substituted back on!

The shift in momentum has Zoe flustered. And when she's flustered, she gets physical. And mouthy. "We're better off without you," she says. "Just look at us dominating you."

"Game's not over yet," you fire back.

Turn the page.

Moments later, the Badger right winger races past midfield with the ball. She passes up to Zoe, who dribbles towards the goal. You rush over to meet her.

"Behind you!" Steffi calls out. But your focus is on Zoe. You're determined to stop her.

To heed Steffi's warning, go to page 81.
To ignore Steffi and head for Zoe, turn to page 93.

Zoe is your focus. But you can't ignore Steffi's warning. She literally has your back.

You glance over your shoulder. A second Badger is racing up behind you. You skid to a stop, your studs catching in the grass. The Badger brushes past you, narrowly missing a collision.

As you stop, Zoe passes the ball. You twist your body towards it and lash out a leg.

Thump.

You intercept the pass, hearing Zoe draw in her breath sharply. You pass the ball to Luna, who sends it past midfield.

The pass reaches Malia, and the Jaguars send the ball around, confusing and confounding the Badger defenders until Hannah is able to sneak a goal past Mara.

Turn the page.

She's levelled the game! You glance up at the clock. There's just over a minute left!

The Badgers get the ball. Their defender kicks it high and wide, and it sails past midfield like an incoming rocket. It's arcing down right at you! From the corner of your eye, you see Zoe coming towards you.

To wait for the ball to come down, turn to page 94.
To jump up to head the ball, turn to page 95.

You see Steffi stumble, and Luna is too far away. You know that Zoe is the Badgers' best player, but that doesn't mean you should ignore the other attacking players on the pitch. You slide to your right to defend against the pass.

Zoe sees this too and takes the shot herself.

Jasmine shuffles left, and the ball lands squarely in her waiting arms. It's an awesome save, and it reminds you that if you're going to win, you'll have to trust your new teammates.

The Jaguars score a couple of goals in the first half, taking the lead. But that doesn't sit well with the Badgers. They were playing aggressively at the start of the match. Now they're being downright brutal.

The right winger sweeps for the ball and takes out Steffi at the legs.

Turn the page.

Tweep! The ref gives a free kick.

Zoe shoves Luna from behind.

Tweep! Another foul.

It's getting rough.

Zoe brings the ball down the pitch. While you want to be as aggressive as she is, you know it's better to hang back. She goes to pass the ball, and you see the other Badger is wide open.

To stick with covering Zoe, go to page 85.
To turn and play for the pass, turn to page 96.

Keep your eyes on Zoe, you tell yourself.

She passes the ball, just as you expected. And you're there to intercept it. The ball flips into the air. You jump up and kick it with all your strength past midfield.

Turn the page.

Malia takes the ball and tries to score, but the Badgers goalkeeper blocks her shot. At the end of the first half, your team has a one-goal lead.

But the Badgers aren't giving up without a fight. The second half is rough and relentless. They aren't backing down or giving up any more goals, which makes your job as a defender that much harder.

After a great save by Mara Rinehart, the Badger goalkeeper, your opponents bring the ball up the pitch. Zoe leads the way, taking a pass from the left winger. She's got a clear shot at the goal.

You race over. There's a chance you can stop her. But should you take it?

To let Zoe go free towards the goal, go to page 87.
To try to intercept Zoe, turn to page 97.

Zoe is about to shoot. She draws her foot back.

You consider diving in front of the ball, but that's risky. So you let Jasmine try to make the save. Unfortunately, Zoe is too good. The Badger striker slips it past Jasmine to level the score!

The two teams battle through extra time, neither getting the advantage over the other. When the whistle blows, the score is still level.

"It's a shoot-out," Coach Stevens says.

"Let me go first," Hannah offers.

This may be your time to shine, though. You consider asking Coach Stevens if you can go first.

But should you?

To suggest that you kick first, turn to page 98.
To let Hannah kick first, turn to page 100.

You're no newbie – you played alongside Zoe and know this move. She's going to fake a pass and take the shot herself.

You race up to her . . .

And she boots the ball to the other Badger!

You've misjudged the play, and the winger easily scores. The Badgers' lead is strong, and there's little time left. You've basically just handed them the win.

"Looks like it's game over," Zoe says.

And sadly, she's right.

THE END

To follow another path, turn to page 11.
To learn more about football, turn to page 103.

Do you want to join the attack too and maybe score the vital goal yourself? You bet you do.

You follow Jamine up the pitch.

The Jaguars have a corner kick. Malia takes it, sending the ball high and in your direction. This is it! You leap up to head the ball towards the goal – but a Badger defender does the same thing! She beats you to it, knocking the ball away. Zoe scoops it up and delivers a kick that sails into the open net at the other end just as the whistle blows.

It's game over, and the Jaguars have lost. You wish you had stayed defending. Maybe then the outcome would have been different.

THE END

To follow another path, turn to page 11.
To learn more about football, turn to page 103.

You'd love to play attack. But that open goal behind you is scary. So you opt to stay defending.

And it's a good thing too. As Malia takes a corner kick, a Badger deflects it with her head. The ball lands near Zoe, who boots it towards the open goal.

Just before it slides over the goal line, you race over and intercept the shot. You quickly pass forward to Luna, who sends it to Bao past midfield.

Seconds remain. Time is running out!

Bao hurries up the pitch. You watch nervously. "Come on," you whisper.

Bao passes to Hannah, and just as time runs out, Hannah sends a shot that sails past the Badger goalie. The game is level!

Turn the page.

In extra time, the momentum is clearly with the Jaguars. Jasmine goes back to her goal. After a stellar stop, she lobs the ball past midfield to Malia.

Malia bends a kick that the Badger goalkeeper was not expecting.

Swish!

It strikes the back of the net.

"Jaguars win!" the ref shouts.

You join your team in midfield to celebrate your amazing, come-from-behind victory!

THE END

To follow another path, turn to page 11.
To learn more about football, turn to page 103.

Steffi is shouting, but you barely hear her. Zoe is your primary focus.

As you reach her, though, the Badger left winger comes up behind you. You barely see her before she collides with you. You tangle limbs, and you both fall hard to the ground.

Pain ripples through your ankle. It's twisted.

"Let me help you," Steffi says. She takes your hand, and you try to stand. But applying too much pressure is agonizing.

You should have listened to Steffi. Because you didn't, the Badgers end up with the win, and your season is probably over due to injury.

THE END

To follow another path, turn to page 11.
To learn more about football, turn to page 103.

In this situation, a header is dangerous. You're not going to risk it.

Zoe doesn't think that way, though. As the ball comes down, she leaps up and hits it squarely with her chest. The ball rolls harmlessly away as the whistle blows.

In extra time, the Badgers get the ball on the counter-attack. Zoe fools Jasmine and sends the game-winning shot past the Jaguar goalkeeper.

The Badgers have won, and you can only watch as they celebrate on the pitch.

THE END
To follow another path, turn to page 11.
To learn more about football, turn to page 103.

Zoe isn't going to back down, and neither will you. It's a risky move, but you jump into the air.

Whump!

The ball strikes you on the crown of your head, sailing past Zoe and right to Bao!

Bao takes the ball up the pitch. Seconds remain.

She shoots and scores!

The crowd goes wild! The Jaguars have won with a last-minute goal! And your risky move was crucial in the victory!

THE END

To follow another path, turn to page 11.
To learn more about football, turn to page 103.

Zoe is going to pass. You've been her teammate, so you know her moves. And so you turn to face the other Badger.

Zoe does pass the ball. But as she does, she bumps into you. You stumble forward, bracing your fall with your hands.

As you hit the grass, your left wrist tweaks. Pain shoots up your arm and into your fingertips.

You jog to the sidelines, clutching your injured wrist.

"Looks like you're sitting this one out," Coach Stevens says. She hands you an ice pack.

You can only watch as the Badgers come back and win.

THE END
To follow another path, turn to page 11.
To learn more about football, turn to page 103.

Zoe is about to shoot. You see her draw her foot back.

There isn't much time. You dive feet-first, sliding across the grass in front of her.

The kick sails forward and strikes you right in the nose. You feel a wave of pain, and your vision blurs as your eyes water.

While you're down, the Badger winger takes a shot. And since Jasmine is distracted by you, the ball sails past her.

Coach Stevens comes to help you off the pitch. Your nose is throbbing. "It's not broken," she says, "but you'll have to come off."

You sit on the sidelines, waiting for the pain to stop, as the Badgers beat your new team.

THE END

To follow another path, turn to page 11.
To learn more about football, turn to page 103.

"I can take the first penalty, Coach," you say before Hannah can ask again.

Coach Stevens looks at Hannah. Hannah nods. "It's her old team," she says. "Makes sense."

Coach Stevens agrees. "Now let's go out there and win."

You're the first of five Jaguars to take a penalty. Mara crouches and stretches as you place the ball and line up your shot.

Thwack!

You send it sailing to her left, but Mara dives, deflecting the ball and saving your penalty!

You see Zoe smirking. "Nice try," she mouths to you.

This wasn't the plan. And it only gets worse. The Badgers score three penalties, and the Jaguars only manage two. You've lost the match.

THE END

To follow another path, turn to page 11.
To learn more about football, turn to page 103.

You'd like to take the first penalty. But you're new to the team, and Hannah is their leader.

"Show us the way, Hannah," you say, bumping fists with her.

Hannah does just that! She sneaks the first penalty past Mara.

When it's your turn, you line up as if you're going to do the opposite of Hannah. But then you do the same thing. You score!

The Jaguars end up scoring four of the five penalties. Jasmine saves three of the five Badger kicks, sealing your victory!

THE END
To follow another path, turn to page 11.
To learn more about football, turn to page 103.

CHAPTER 5

A WORLDWIDE SPORT

Football is one of the world's oldest sports. Its history dates to a game played with a ball more than 2,000 years ago in China. By the 1100s, the game had spread to England. It involved kicking a ball, but wasn't much like today's game.

Today, two teams of 11 players compete on a pitch with goal nets at each end. One player from each team, called a goalkeeper, guards each net. The players on the pitch use their feet, torsos and even their heads to pass the ball. They try to get the ball into the opposing team's net and score a goal. Only the goalkeepers are allowed to touch the ball with their hands.

The version of football we know began in England in 1863. Several English football teams united and formed the Football Association (FA).

As the sport developed, rules were added. The FA was an amateur league, meaning the players weren't paid. That changed in the late 1800s, as England and other countries created professional leagues. By 1900, football was being played around the world.

The Fédération Internationale de Football Association (FIFA) formed in 1904. FIFA oversees the sport on a global level. In 1908, football was officially included in the Olympic Games. FIFA hosted the first World Cup in 1930. In 1996, women's football became part of the Olympics.

Football is the best-known sport internationally. In the 1990s, its popularity began to grow in the United States, where this story is set, thanks in part to its hosting of the 1994 FIFA World Cup.

Today, Major League Soccer (MLS), the professional men's league in North America, has 26 teams. Three are in Canada and the rest are in the United States. The LA Galaxy is the most successful MLS team, with five MLS Cup titles.

Football is especially popular with girls in the United States. The National Women's Soccer League formed in 2012, and as of 2020 it had nine professional women's teams. On an international level, the United State's women's team has had great success. The team has won four gold medals and one silver medal in the Olympics and four World Cups, the last in 2019.

GLOSSARY

card when players commit fouls they can be shown either
a yellow or red card. Yellow cards are given as a caution,
while red cards mean the player must leave the pitch.

forward player who plays nearest to the opponent's goal net;
also called a sriker

header when the head is used to pass, shoot, block or
otherwise control the ball

midfielder player generally positioned on the pitch between
the defenders and forwards

shoot-out method used after extra time, when a match
cannot end in a draw, to decide who wins. Teams take
turns having penalty kicks.

striker forward whose main job is to score goals

throw-in when the ball goes out of play, the opposing team
of the team who last touched the ball is allowed to throw
the ball onto the pitch

wingback player who plays in a wide position on the pitch,
taking part both in attack and defence

TEST YOUR FOOTBALL KNOWLEDGE

1. Who is the only player on the pitch allowed to touch the ball with his or her hands?

    A. striker

    B. goalkeeper

    C. forward

2. How many people play at one time on a football team?

    A. 10

    B. 9

    C. 11

3. What is another name for football?

    A. soccer

    B. foot game

    C. affiliated goals

4. What is football's international championship called?

    A. World Series

    B. Football Championship

    C. World Cup

5. How is a football match started?

    A. tip-off

    B. throw-in

    C. kick-off

6. What are the players who play closest to the opposing goal called?

    A. forwards

    B. midfielders

    C. wingbacks

7. What piece of equipment are players required to wear in an organized game of football?

    A. mouth guard

    B. shin pads

    C. gloves

8. Which throw-in would be considered improper?

   A. the player jumps while throwing the ball

   B. the player throwing the ball uses both hands

   C. the player throwing the ball throws it from over his or her head

9. What is the box around the goal called?

   A. goal box

   B. hands-free zone

   C. penalty box

10. If an attacking player is fouled inside the penalty box, the result is a _____.

   A. corner kick

   B. penalty kick

   C. direct kick

DISCUSSION QUESTIONS

>>> Describe a time when you joined a new team or played against a team with your friends on it. How did it feel?

>>> You are writing an article for the school's website about the Jaguars. Choose one outcome and describe it from your perspective. Did the Jaguars win or lose?

>>> What is your favourite sporting moment? How did you feel when it happened?

>>> Write about a time your team won an important game. Now write about a time you lost a game. Share the differences in how you felt during each experience.

AUTHOR BIOGRAPHY

Brandon Terrell is the author of numerous books and graphic novels, ranging from sports stories to spooky tales to mind-boggling mysteries. When not hunched over his laptop writing, Brandon enjoys watching films and television, reading, cooking and spending time with his wife and two children in Minnesota, USA.

ILLUSTRATOR BIOGRAPHY

Fran Bueno was born and lives in Santiago de Compostela in Spain. Since he was a small child, he has loved comic books. He was reading *El Jabato* at the age of eight, a comic book that his father always bought him, and in that exact moment he decided to become an artist. He studied at art school and will always be grateful to his parents for supporting him. His motivation is to do what he does best and enjoys most. He loves travelling with his wife and kids, being with friends, books, music, films and TV shows. Just a regular guy? He would agree.

YOU CHOOSE BOOKS IN THIS SERIES!

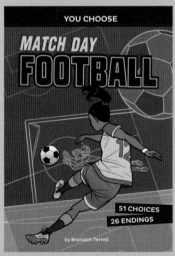